UNBUILT PROJECTS

ALSO BY PAUL LISICKY

Lawnboy
Famous Builder
The Burning House

UNBUILT PROJECTS

Paul Lisicky

Four Way Books
Tribeca

Please direct all inquiries to:
Editorial Office
Four Way Books
POB 535, Village Station
New York, NY 10014
www.fourwaybooks.com

Library of Congress Cataloging-in-Publication Data

Lisicky, Paul.
[Prose works. Selections]
Unbuilt projects / Paul Lisicky.
    pages cm
ISBN 978-1-935536-25-3 (pbk. : alk. paper)
I. Title.
PS3562.I773U53 2012
818'.5403--dc23

                                2012002013

This book is manufactured in the United States of America
and printed on acid-free paper.

Four Way Books is a not-for-profit literary press. We are grateful for the assistance
we receive from individual donors, public arts agencies, and private foundations.

This publication is made possible with public funds
from the National Endowment for the Arts

and from the New York State Council on the Arts, a state agency.

We are a proud member
of the Council of Literary Magazines and Presses.

Distributed by University Press of New England
One Court Street, Lebanon, NH 03766

CONTENTS

For my mother, in memory.

"The house does not seem big enough to hold all the people who keep appearing in it at different times."

Lydia Davis, "The Strangers"

PALO ALTO

Maybe it was the smell of cough drop on the air. And the trees:
eucalyptus, birch, palm, redwood, side by side in one space. It
might have been the thinking inside the houses I passed, minds
at work over desks, fingers tapping keys, tapping foreheads.
Maybe it was the nearness of the sea. And the mountain
between the highway and the sea, levels inside landscape, inside
moments: wholeness the lie we always suspected it was, and
we could finally get down to this business of motion, of making
ourselves up again. I ran faster than I'd ever run before. My feet
flew over this pavement and that. I went all the way past the
stable. And when I took that shortcut past the schoolyard—the
children inside with their tom-toms—I thought of what they'd be
when they were running past these windows.

Fifty minutes passed. Or years? A live oak sagged through
a kitchen ceiling. A parachute hung out to dry, in pieces. And
when I asked the men in the sport coats where the town was, I
knew they knew as much as I did. Wasn't that where they dump
the ashes? one said. The toys, said his friend. The ashes and the
toys, said the first. Their shoes hovered just above the ground,

and when the wind picked up, they knocked into each other, gently, like paper lanterns with hooks on top.

So I shouldn't have been surprised to see the ghosts. Oh, they weren't ghosts, not exactly, but two girls, seven or so, who leapt out behind the parked car. "Hello!" they cried out in glee. "Hello! Hello!" They of course didn't know I'd been at this for a while. No wallet, no phone, no driver's license, no GPS. Not even a permanent house to return to, just one more set of rooms, chairs so durable and featureless you'd never known they'd been holding you up. I nodded and walked on. But the little girls? You stopped to play tag when you were picked on, even if you couldn't walk, even if the fear in you smelled of mushrooms. "Hello," they said again, this time with an ache in it. "Hello! Hello! Hello!" The trees ahead of me shook their crowns. They started coming nearer, smiles as bright as toxins. Was that happiness seeping through my shoes—or just another trap? Into the garden I went. A man knelt beside a pond, forearm thrust all the way to the bottom, hand working through the gold and the slop as if life itself depended on it. A jar, a pot, a bottle, another pot. So many lost things, tangled with grasses, rinsed clean by the action of the clear, cold air. "Could I help?" I said, but they were already upon us. I turned around to greet them: *I am not your enemy.* And when he pulled me up from the muck, the light in me gushed forth.

THE BOY AND HIS MOTHER ARE STUCK!

If I'd been the kind of seven-year-old who turned up in stories, I might have said to her, "Listen, after we get out of this, we'll get ourselves to a good cafeteria, order two tapiocas with cherries on top, and laugh and laugh about the idiots we made of ourselves." Instead, I rested my head on the pretend steering wheel beside her real steering wheel and wept. I wept and I wept, careful to match my sobs to hers, careful not to outpace her in misery. She didn't lift her head, and I didn't lift my head. Our eyes burned in fury, in frustration. If you'd read about us in a story, you might not have seen yourself reflected in us. You might have said, that woman needs some pluck, a little sass: what is she, some kind of actress, a victim? And that son of hers?

But this wasn't any story. We were stuck in the snow, in the woods, on a one-way lane, many years ago when the world was getting darker. The sky was getting darker. We'd made some wrong turns. The empty lot we were looking for wasn't anywhere in sight, just like the big house we'd hoped to build on it was only a picture in our heads. One life was coming to an end: a baby on the way any minute. (Boy? Girl? My mother had

wanted a girl. She'd made that clear to us.) And as if to prove
to us the old house was no longer adequate, the windows were
leaking air, and a smell of rotten plants wafted from the pond in
the backyard.

Would I miss the old house? Not if she didn't.

Just yesterday, when we were all a little calmer and safer, my
younger brother put his palms on the oven of her and murmured
duck, duck, I want a duck as if words alone could make the thing
inside her grow feathers.

"Show me the joy in childhood!" demanded the writing
teacher, sometime between that time and where we are now.
And he squeezed his fist on the tabletop and said what he had to
say as if he were trying to convince himself of the truest thing.
And he looked at me with wise, demented eye as if he wanted to
punch the look off my face. And all I can say, today, is Joy, visit
me now.

And him.

But that wasn't the life inside the car. Inside, my mother turned
the wheel to the left, gunned the accelerator, and turned. She

tried it again. Left, right, left, right, and left again. Little by little we sank in it and slid. We edged forward. The road was behind us now, on top of us, higher than our heads. And the harder she turned, the darker went our wishes. We were inside the dream of it now, the rash, irrepressible dream; we were already on the way, and it wasn't as awful as you'd think. And need I say that the trees reared like deer ready to take us in, and need I say that we were closer to bliss than anything we'd ever known? "Give me the strength," my mother whispered, and the grip in her voice was so tight that I knew the duck, if it chose to, wanted to, could fly out the open space between her legs. And it wouldn't be the friendly duck my brother wanted. No, it wouldn't be the duck that would save us, but it would fly round and round our heads, knocking the windshield with its beak, looking for a way out.

And just when I was certain our separate skins had become one, my mind shifted and sprung, even though it took me years to give it words.

You are you and I am me.

What? (Though no one actually said this.)

You are you. I don't have to feel this.

And I fell through the trap of the story with, what? A duck in my arms. Sweet duck, of the lightest weight, pressing her neck to my neck. And if I stayed still long enough, and breathed, tuning myself to her pulse, I knew she'd take me up with her.

And let me go when it was time.

I was thinking on that a little while when the tow truck came. A tiny black man stepped through a hole in the pines, and without much trouble at all, pulled the car out of the snow with a heavy clinking chain that left a grease mark on the white.

I stood behind the car after it was over, rubbing the bumper as if to cure it.

And if only that were the end, and the story didn't insist on telling itself again.

THE PHYSICS OF THE KNOWN WORLD

That silly retriever. He doesn't go to the two guys looking right
at him, beaming him awake with concentrated joy. Not at all: he
goes straight to the man with his head turned to the left, who
could care less about doggy behavior and isn't the least bit stirred
by the snout parked in the knee and the wagging hind parts.
And that's it: the physics of the known world. Which is why
the trees look better when they're left unwatered, and the birds
actually prefer it when you don't sing back to them. And the
holy man crossing the street with the black brim hat? He knows
better than to pick up what he's dropped and lift his face to the
mountains. Take it from him, friend. You probably wouldn't even
want it if the light hit you in your head.

THE ROOFERS

Outside, by the front deck, the roofers are laughing again. They pretend that they don't see me through the window. I pretend that I don't hear them at my desk. I like the roofers. I'm happy to give them water when they ask for it; I like watching the guard go down in their eyes when they take their cups. I don't even mind when they play their boombox too loud, and the sounds of "American Woman" pull my attention out to the patio, where the sawhorses are set up. Even their jokes interest me. *Do you like it when I hold my crotch when I talk to you?* one says. *Not as much as when I have my lips on your butt,* says another. And I'm practically laughing along. And though they'll drive home to their wives and girlfriends once the four o'clock ferry pulls into the dock on the mainland, they're not afraid in the least of what's in front of them. The roofers: just look at the way they start goofing when "Dancing Queen" comes on.

Sun on skin, hot gold light frying the hydrangea. Is this how it happens? I mean, change, here, in a yard. Laughter taken into one ear, then returned, and passed on to another and another. And as for the old excuse of setting one man out to make the

11

other men in? Well, we're over that.

I think I might be seeing what I want to see. I think I still want to believe in the God of my childhood, who was reminded, in song, that he'd champion the peacemaker. I think I don't want to hear the military plane on its daily route just over the beach. I don't even want to know about the deer who stepped up to the stranger for a bite of his apple today. *First he fed him half his apple*, the roofer mutters, *and then he shot him in the head.* Sun on the floor. Tang of smoke in the nose and the eye. I freeze, as if the ghost of that animal's slipped in and out of the house, before I catch myself edging forward on the seat. A part of me wants more: death, death, the low, delicious word, whispered to me through night.

And then I roll my chair to the corner of the room.

The gun going off, the body magnificent slumping to the forest floor. Who wants to hear it? Haven't we had enough? And what of the guy's girlfriend who might cover her ears when he lets her in on his secret, later tonight, after a bout of good sex?

I don't know about that, I don't know about that.

I want a smile to do all the work for me. I want to smile and smile and smile my bright American smile.

Outrage? Oh, I have it—and plenty. Don't you? But it lasts as long as the next e-mail comes in.

Virginia Woolf says, "But sympathy we cannot have. Wisest Fate says no. If her children, weighted as they already are with sorrow, were to take on them that burden too . . . buildings would cease to rise; roads would peter out into grassy tracks. . . ."

But we all know what she did once the enemy planes started flying too low over the downs. Halfway to her waist in the mud. That's right, behind the house she loved.

Help us. The wheels on this chair, the roofers overhead, my shoes, the spent fuel that keeps us running—I can't think too long on the cost of what it took to get them here without the whole operation shutting down. The deer licks the salt from my hand. I don't even know what to ask for any more; it's that mixed up. Teach me what to ask, if I may still call you by your name. Water in the mouth: Teach me, sir.

THIS IS THE DAY

1. HOW'S FLORIDA?

And life, for one shining moment, in the summer, at the shore house, was almost golden.

But not before the forgetting. The big red forgetting machine, not exactly asked for, but certainly willing to get the job done. And what might you drop down its spout? Think: one suicide, one car crash, two violent deaths, one crazy cousin, miscarriage 1, miscarriage 2, miscarriage 3, one lecherous boss . . . Sweet Jesus, let's spare one another the facts: her life, my life. This is meant to be the story of all lives, though I'm talking about one in particular. The point is, the damn thing made it possible for my mother to live, and now I'm standing in its spray, using whatever it took in to mulch my garden.

See how the plants grow.

And die a little.

"But we've all heard this story before," says the moss beneath the rock. "If you're interested in the march of time, or in how things morph and grow, why not consider . . . evolution."

Evolution? The march of time? Well, then.

On an otherwise unremarkable morning in Florida, my mother walks to her dining room table, where I've been sitting, stops, beams at me, and says, "you almost feel like my son." But I am your son, I answer, laughing warily, as if in response to a punch line that's a little off. "Then you must be my twin," she says. And when I think, but Paul's been dead for sixty years, she asks whether I went to school with him. And back and forth goes the Q&A, as calm as calm could be, until we're both weary of the lesson. And just when I think I've pulled her back by the rope of my talk to a place we thought familiar, she asks, "Who are your brothers and sisters?" But she isn't satisfied with the two grown men's names I say aloud. "Hon," she says to my father. "Hon." My father, who's half-looking at the electric bill, half-listening to the portable TV on the countertop. "Hon, Paul is our son." And the slightest look of hurt in his eyes suggests that *he's* been the one who's been exposed. *He's* been the one in the wrong. And she keeps laughing, shy and a little pleased to be at the center of things. "I'm sorry," she says. "I'm so, so sorry. You're my sweetheart."

I'm 45 years old, I almost say, *and you're just being born.*

Three days later, after I was no longer frozen, or more interested than broken, I was sorry too. Not just for what you're thinking, but for the words I whispered as I was falling asleep that night: *She's leaving us. She likes someone better than us. And here I'd thought we meant everything. She wants to play with the monkeys. Holy, holy, holy, sing the monkeys. Blessed is she who comes in the name of the Lord.*

So the impulse that helps you live ends up doing you in. That's it in a nutshell, right? That's what I'm supposed to learn?

Hosanna in the Highest.

"And how's Florida?" says my friend, Luis, though he's not exactly asking about a travel destination.

And I don't have it in me to tell him that she wasn't on my mind.

2. PAUL ALL GONE

No cry, no moan—easy as a crown rolling out onto a bed of blankets. That's the story I've made of my mother's story. I mean, her version of the time her twin fell out of the car. And what did her father say to the empty space on the seat when he finally looked over his shoulder?

"Where's Paul?"

"Paul all gone," said my mother.

As if that were the funniest thing. Though she couldn't have known it was funny until she heard her father tell it, and she saved the story by making someone laugh. Paul, it should be noted, was okay—at least for then. My grandfather turned the car around, stopped, and scooped him up in his arms. Though much later, Paul wasn't. And you probably know that his ending had something to do with a car.

The way my mother told it, the first incident didn't prefigure the next. She kept the two stories apart. That way, she could still make you laugh and come out winning.

But even the five-year-old me couldn't take out the bad story from the good.

And what of the naughty gleam turned to me this morning, her memory long asleep, a lost child in the woods beside the road?

Paul all gone? I almost say for her.

But her face says it instead. My mother: she still has it in her to be funny.

3. A PHONE CALL WITH MY FATHER

"Maybe that's the way to go," my father says. "All at once you're flat on your back and speechless, listening to your upstairs neighbor go on."

"What exactly did you say to her?" I say.

He pauses, as if he's trying to ground himself, before acting it out, as a storyteller would. "I said, 'Listen. Ethel. You're going to see your mother, your father, and your husband soon. Your older sister, and the cat you used to feed. Everyone you ever knew and missed.' And she gripped my hand as hard as she could and looked me straight in the eye.' And that was that. And wouldn't you know that's when the stupid ambulance pulls up."

"And you're sure she wanted to see these people? What if she couldn't stand her mother?"

But I should be quiet already. The truth is, I'm wondering where *he's* gone. Where's the father who used to insist that when you're dead you're dead, even as he took us, week after week, to church?

"What's religion have to do with it?"

"I'm just saying I think it's important that what you say in that kind of situation be exactly right. Not everyone believes in a Heaven."

"Okay, Mister You-Have-All-the-Answers. Who'd *you* want to see?"

And that stops me. Not because I can't begin to form the words I'd want to make, and not because I'm stumped (this face and that face come flying toward me like snow) but because she's right there with him in the next room, waiting for him to bring her a cup of something warm. But it isn't my father my mother wants, not the man she's lived with fifty-one years, but Lulu or Bernice, or whatever new name she'll give him tonight. And I'd be lying to you if my father and I don't shake our heads and laugh some about this, especially on a good day, when her neck isn't hurting, or when she isn't talking too much about her mother, and how she'd be able to see her if she just had the energy to walk to the other side of the road.

Is that how we want to go, with most of our memory scraped? Think of how it was to live just seconds after we entered the world. Our senses so raw, they couldn't get enough of things.

This is the day the Lord has made.

Now I wonder if I'd recognize her if I saw her again. I mean the old mother. Walking down the highway with suitcase in hand. Would she even stop to talk if I said hello?

Maybe we all made her up, that lady who shared our house, and put on red lipstick, and told us she was proud of us.

"Aside from her," my father says finally, quiet now, as if trying to make things simpler.

*

Sometime before the first life became the next life—though there were never really two lives, even as we talk about them like that—my mother walked up to him with wonder and alarm in her eyes. "What is it, Hon?" he said, startled, without the old impatience we'd grown so used to. "You look funny." And it was true: her green eyes looked clearer than they'd looked in weeks. Without even waiting for her reply, he knew she knew there was a stranger in her kitchen. And though she might have said, "get out of my house," she reached for his hand and held it. They stood like that for a while, leaning into the refrigerator, nodding, as she pressed that hand to her side. And though I know not the details, and know not the new name she called him, I picture my father leading my mother down the hall past the place where the piano used to be. And the story of whatever happened inside the bedroom carried them together for a long, long time, even after things got worse, even after my mother started telling people in the lobby of her building, with an exhilarated hush, "a man has moved into our apartment and I think I really like him."

Fifty-one years of arguments: gone like that.

And Jesus appeared before him with his shining body: *Put your hand into my side if you believe.*

WHAT MIGHT LIFE BE LIKE IN THE 21ˢᵗ CENTURY ?

Sleek black hair. Blue, blue eyes. No other reason she'd have talked to Mr. Science, who would have looked past her to the other mothers even if I'd built an atom smasher behind the school. The topic of discussion was my science fair project, "What Might Life Be Like in the 21ˢᵗ Century." I'd waited until the night before to throw it all together, as I'd done with every homework assignment that year, out of some protest I couldn't put a name to. What was the point of saying the here-and-now was good for us? My protest must have shown up in everything I did, from my matted hair, to my refusal to speak a word in class, to my walking off the field whenever I saw a fly ball coming in my direction. I was ready to go to sleep, though I hadn't even started my day. So no surprise Mr. Science led my mother to the corner of the cafeteria, sat her down away from the other mothers, and told her, in a slow, deep voice, that he saw no future for the likes of me.

What was it like to take in those words? Did it hurt to hear them? Did they excite her? Or did she relax into the hot scratchy wool of her skirt as a patient might listen to the gravest diagnosis? No wonder my perfected city didn't look like the other projects on the table. No wonder she couldn't take in the shiny houses I'd drawn without wanting to head for the door. And in that moment, when it was still possible to turn back, she might have wanted to touch Mr. Science's face. Instead, she turned her head and saved herself from that apology. She looked out toward the other mothers, tried to picture herself among them, happy and glistening, and listened to what she could of his words.

"Science fair projects," he said, with an easy, cruel smile curving his mouth, "are about proving what's already known and finding the evidence to support those claims. I have to be honest with you. That's not what I'm seeing in your son's project."

"And his grade?" she said, with hope, as if she hadn't even heard the half of it.

"Well," he said, and held up two hands, letting them hang in the air. "If I give him an F, maybe it'll teach him a thing or two."

"Thank you," she said, and stood up. She gathered her scarf

and gloves. And drove home, calming herself by counting the trees along the way, as if she'd finally found the key to help me live.

What could I say to her delivery, her looking about the living room—chair to table to desk to chair—as if its proportions had become more spacious in her absence? She sat down across from me, face shining, eyes deadly cool, in the hopes I'd finally get it. I couldn't tell her I didn't care about proof and evidence. That world didn't want us in it, because who among us even had the words to make those claims? That world? That world was a funhouse, full of mirrors reflecting nothing but my tossed-off homework, my drowsing shoulders, the thick, drab poison of me, me, me, me, me. I wanted to be more than that sad little nothing. I wanted to roll in the grass with the animals. The future? So what if it ended up letting us down? I was ready to get there. I was ready to rattle its gates, even if I couldn't see past the houses, parks, and boulevards I'd drawn on that smudged sheet of posterboard.

The future arrived: that much I was sure of. And though it

didn't have the fires and punishments that transfigured their dreams, it did have all those other things, and more. The human touch? She ached for it, starved for it. Why shouldn't she eat the sweet rind she'd been wanting for herself? That must have crossed her mind every time she saw me walking down the street, past the orange trees and the palms, away from her. We knew exactly what it was she deserved, but the city was already ruined.

HINCHCLIFFE

"They say what they think you want them to say."
Richard Hughes, *A High Wind in Jamaica*

We didn't mind crawling through the bushes. Or think about
the change in his face, which had lost the cruelty we'd known
in other children's faces. We followed his lead, as if he were
no longer one of us, but a father, leading us into the fire. First
Joselle Friedman, then Suzy Friedman, the four of us squeezing
between the bushes and the laundry room, inside the shadows
where the mud was soft like pumpkin. We sat on the backs of
our shoes, waiting, a little frightened of what was to come. Our
breaths fell in sync, almost musical. On the other side of the
trees, the others shrieked and piped and played their games, not
even knowing we were gone.

Freeze! someone cried, but it might have come from another life,
from the cold bright world of the rabbits.

And here the story says no. No music, no rapture for those
who've joined us on our travels, for what can be said but that he
pooped? And that stupid word insists upon its presence on the
page, even as the story knows that what we saw was anything

26

but stupid. Head turned to the right, palms pressed to the mud, he did what he did not for himself, really, but for us, as if he were performing a reminder. *The world is much larger than we can say. Don't believe them.* Then the pants went up, one palm brushed against the other palm, and in no time at all we went back to the games of hopscotch and tag, pretending not to have learned that the wires above our heads actually had a mind.

Then the cries went up in the village, though there wasn't any village, only Mrs. Hinchcliffe—yes, the boy had a mother and a name—whose contorted face told us there was a whole body of people inside her, ready to throw stones, trying to get out. And Hinchcliffe scurried away with his pants half down, as if he'd planned it that way, knowing all along that his mother had had to find him.

What do you know about this? said Mrs. Hinchcliffe to us.

Nothing. The three of us stood before her, shoulder to shoulder, as if we'd slaughtered a robin.

How long has this been going on?

We don't know, we said, shaking our heads. But we knew

we were talking as children were supposed to talk, tiny and shameful, though there was a sweetness to the lie.

That was the birthing of the new: that sweetness. Other mothers would follow Mrs. Hinchcliffe's lead: Mrs. Lennox, Mrs. Chalupa. Always something for them to pounce upon, weep about, as if they'd been the ones at fault and we'd been living out what they'd been afraid to want. Nude hospital in the treehouse, bosoms scissored from magazines, until we, too, were walking around with kind and distant faces, professing to care about one another. Who would not want it that way? *We don't know,* we said again and again, until we'd stopped giving them reasons to find us. Then wires were just wires, birds were annoyances, and the lake on the other side of the trees was only something you could drown in.

And Hinchcliffe? For a long time we didn't remember his name.

TWO PIANOS

Though they were old now, and hadn't had a piano in the house they'd left behind, the man's mother and father knew their lives were poorer without music, and they'd found a baby grand, used, a little out of tune. So what if neither of them could play? The man would be along to visit and they knew he couldn't stop. Which was true. The first night he saw it, he put down his suitcase by the front door, walked past the China closet, and slid back the bench. If an outsider had come in, he'd have heard the pedal buzzing beneath the man's foot; he'd have seen the parents move more nimbly above the saucepan or the checkbook. And it didn't matter to them that all he played were fragments, one rhythm shifting into the next. A beginning implied an ending. No one in that house wanted an ending, not with night coming closer. Better to be suspended in the present, like a fern frozen at the bottom of a lake.

The second piano was central to a second house. Another baby grand, also used, this of better make and model. The front entryway demanded Schubert, Liszt, for who knew who would walk in the door? This was the house of adulthood. These were the rooms he shared with his lover, and as such, there was no time for scraps or fragments. This life called for order, artifact, a narrative with an arc and a shape. But an arc and a shape wanted an ending, and an ending implied evaluation—if not someone else's then his own. All the lures of achievement, and was that beyond the range of the man's wishes? Still, he'd never forget the way he'd been surprised that Christmas. And the look on his lover's face when he pulled off the bedspread and was told he could open his eyes. Every time he thought of that face, the gladness around the mouth and the chin, the man wanted to play a song that equaled it, though he didn't know what.

But the fact was he didn't. The fact was he played both pianos less and less, and passed them by on the way to what was next.

Was it that he didn't want to acknowledge that practice was in order, and his high school piano teacher was onto something when she pointed out the way his hands had fallen on the keys? Maybe he simply didn't want to admit that he'd been a little too easy on himself and he had more work to do. Art is hard, and he didn't want to be reminded of that old saw.

But that's crap.

He didn't want to know that the air you once thrived in could be loved a little less. He didn't want to know that something else would come to bear him aloft, high above the tar and the waste. The world would go on without it—and him. The next thing would be beautiful. That was a good thing, wasn't it?

Then again it wasn't.

Once it became clear that music wouldn't fill the rooms again, the pollen settled on the keys; the wires went out of tune. And it wasn't the end of the world when decisions were made, in calm, reasonable voices, to let the pianos go. A piano takes up space. A piano makes it harder to move on, and it was better, the man agreed, for the pianos to be where they were wanted, which is where they ended up, one with an old lady who played hers facing the bromeliads in the trees, the other with a five-year-old who wouldn't be pried from the bench, even when he was summoned for ice cream.

And time, as it always was, is the champion of youth.

And he still didn't want an ending.

THE END OF ENGLAND

"The curtain would rise. What would the first words be?"
Virginia Woolf, *Between the Acts*

The townspeople in the novel sit as patiently as schoolchildren, puzzling at the outdoor pageant on the lawn. Wouldn't they rather be in motion, walking through a forest, taking part in that view beyond the birches? Take Miss La Trobe, the director. Nothing would please her more than to spend the evening in the cottage she shares with the actress, no quarrels, just the two of them taking tea, or rubbing each others' feet through their socks. Instead, she must live as if the silences in the play might mean the death of the town. No one's told her, of course, that the town doesn't need her at all. The town's a construction of the author, who must make the story bearable, if only because its language is coming to pieces in front of our eyes. Not just its language but the history of England itself, which is why the pageant's divided into three parts, representing three distinct eras of literary history. The German planes were flying over the writer's house as the book was coming together; no surprise that those same planes fly over the pageant in its final minutes. As for the cheerful tone of the book? What else should we expect when we're saying goodbye to a world we've loved so well?

I'm not halfway through the novel when an older woman bangs down the aisle of the plane. The pilot's about to take off, but that doesn't stop her from making a scene. "No one talks to me like that," she says, in a voice we can barely understand. "No one talks to me like that!" The book's shut for now, not because I no longer care about the end of England, but because the play coming undone in the novel could never compete with the woman coming undone in front of our eyes. She refuses to stay quiet, even after three flight attendants gather round to calm her down. Women her age don't behave like this; at least that's what we've always been told. And maybe that's why she's ferocious, why she's not to be appeased, why she stands up, unbuckling her seatbelt, just as the plane's lifting off the ground to cry, "Greek is the root of English!" She's forgotten something, though she can't seem to figure out what it is. Her luggage? Her name? Where might that lost word be hiding? Under her seat? She's inconsolable, she's reaching into her bag for lipstick, handkerchief, breath mint, brush. She's smoothing out her paisley skirt. And then—silence. Silence and peace. Her eyelids are drowsing. Her head tilts to one side, mouth parting. Maybe she'll sleep now, maybe we'll finally get back to the books on our tray tables, or concentrate on the Florida ahead of us, the soft air on our arms, the smells of wet foliage, sprinkler system, laundry room, and warm swimming pool. Anesthesia and menace: palms creaking against the night. Certainly that outburst would have taken the wind out of a younger person, and she'll wake up to say, what? What was I thinking? Instead, she turns to the person across from me, asks if she could take her hand, and when that person gives in, if only because she doesn't want to stir the woman up again, we hear customs, security. So that's it, customs, security: two words crashing, solving. The woman's voice drops, calm now, indignant, as if she's talking not to us, but to a band of schoolchildren. "This is America. This does not happen in America." And though we don't doubt that she's been wanded and scolded and wanded and scolded again, we also think, this is what you've come to tell us? This is news? Haven't we been so patient, so good? You who could have been our messenger. I'll open my book instead, and sink there, where at least the voice is sweet as it comes undone, where at least one might still hold a whole town inside him—the village idiot, Deb the maid, a duke, a priest, a shepherd—as the engines hum out of sight, just over the rain clouds.

I count the heads in the seats in front of me. Out the window, the farmhouses look so small against the green I'm surprised no one has taken them down yet.

TWO TALES

1. BEAR WEEK

I'm going to hate the way this sounds, but let's get it out of the way: an ugly man sits down beside me on the bench while I'm talking on the phone to Mark. And while I know you're probably shaking your head at "ugly" (not to mention, where is the compassion?) I'll just say that he leans into me with a boozy smile and reaches up into my shorts for the prize. Get it? It doesn't help that this transaction happens while I'm describing the action on the street to Mark, and how do you say, "there's a half-naked man squeezing my dick in public" while tourists are walking by with their ice cream, as if we're just another part of the show? Mark is sounding a little jealous, or more precisely, like he wants some of what I have for himself, and I want to say no, it's not what you think it is, but how can I tell him that the man resembles Uncle Fester, or one of the extraterrestrials from *Close Encounters* minus the charm, without hurting someone? In truth, I don't think the man would be all that bad if he got himself a T-shirt or a personality; if I were a different sort, I'd sit with him until he recovered himself and maybe find out that he, like me, is a Joni Mitchell fan. But who has time for speculation when his hand's all too happy to have found its home, and he's resting his head near the top of my chest like a demented baby about to nurse? Sweet Jesus. Luckily, there's Adam, big Adam, walking down the street, with an unmistakable expression of concern and suppressed horror on his face. Without pause, he summons me over. I put my arm around his shoulder, as if our connection has been long and intimate, and we walk on into the throng, leaving the man to fall sideways into the space where I'd been.

Of course, none of the above would have happened without the handy device of the cellphone, which left me defenseless, although I'd believed it was giving me power, even as it enabled me to put my arm around a man I've somewhat known for years, but had always been a little bit afraid of. But this is not the lesson that you think it is, and my story's not yet coming to a close though it might feel that way, as I'm still talking to Mark, to tell him Adam's come to the rescue. Adam? he says. Adam who? Big Adam. *Big* Adam? he says. And Adam, hearing himself referred to in terms that must flatter him, shifts his arm atop my shoulder to show me how many hours he's been putting in at the gym. And you know what? I kind of like it. No doubt Mark must hear the lifting inside my voice, and Adam must wonder what it feels like to be in Mark's skin right now, itchy and three hundred and sixty-five miles from the tumult and fire of Gay Tourist Town, with your partner under the wing of someone you vaguely know, and the thinnest quaver passes between Adam and me, as if it originated through the phone signal itself, and that's our cue to break apart, and I nod thanks to Adam, say a firm goodbye to Mark, and I'm on my way back to the White Horse Inn.

I'm entertaining myself, telling this sequence of events to myself. One piece in front of the next and back again and back—and isn't it a beautiful night for stories? The sky so scrubbed with stars it hurts. Then a familiar face moving toward me, lit up by the lights outside the pharmacy. Mike, whom I've always liked, but don't know so well. What? he says, looking at what must be the goofy grin on my face. *What?* And how can I not tell him

the story all over again: the boozy smile, the rough wet hand,
big bad Adam, and we both crack up and redden, not because
it's new to me anymore, but—*what?* Beards and dicks and big
daddies careening around us like trucks through waves of water.
And isn't Mike's face looking different than it's ever looked? His
screwy smile, barely concealing his secret animal? And just as
I lean in closer, to tell him I'm going to write this story and put
him in it, I get a hold of myself, cough, and say *so long,* with a
promise to see each other at the reading Saturday night.

And in this way, the ugly man seems to have tied four unlikely
men together by giving us a rope we wouldn't have known we'd
wanted. And made a better thing of the word "ugly" for one
evening. And made us laugh.

Or almost. Ahead—how has he gotten ahead?—he's leaning into
another man on another bench in front of Town Hall. So much
for thinking I was singled out. Up goes the hand into the shorts.
Down goes the corner of the good man's mouth. Where's Adam
when we need him? Where? *There,* in my inbox, twenty-eight

days later, as I'm sitting down to write this story: *I remember that night. I was happy to have helped.*

2. FRIEND

There once was a Paul. Not me, but another Paul whose left ear stuck out more than his right. Not that you'd notice, but Paul certainly noticed. So much so that he wore caps inside and outside, which gave him the air of an aging Italian gentleman, even when he was a teenager. If you really want to disparage yourself, I'd think, you might want to consider your slouch, that mustard-green cardigan, your already fuzzy hairline—my *God.* Of course, I could say those things because I loved him and he didn't love me back. What could be done about two seventeen year old boys, and one whose need was so ferocious that his gaze sent the other backing out the door? When I think about Paul now, I think about the time he confessed, with pants down after awkward sex, to driving his head into the side of his parents' bathtub. Not just once but again and again. And he said it with the smiling resignation that suggested his performance was not to escape the body, even though he finally did escape the body, though not in the way you're thinking.

When the barber pointed out the bump on the back of my head, I didn't lift a finger. Oh, no. I didn't work or wobble it; I didn't stand in front of every three-way mirror I passed looking for signs of growth. I didn't tape it with duct tape; I didn't pour apple cider vinegar onto a cotton ball, which I'd learned could burn the finish off the finest chair. Though I actually did consider the words of the farm boy who sprung open his pocket knife on the second meeting of the writing class: "Do you want me to cut that tick off the back of your head?"

"Let's poke fun at the wounded," said my friend Michael some time later, and I'm still trying to figure out why the whole band of us laughed, and it didn't come off as mean.

Once I read a novel in which a man walked into a remote woods only to find a hermit, quite calm and dignified, who performed plastic surgery on his face with a mirror. The new face wasn't exactly handsome, nor were his stitches remotely transparent, but that was beside the point. Purity, perfection: neither had their place here. We were up to something better. The hermit led the character to a house he'd built with scraps found by the road. He sat the character down in a chair, dropped a teabag into a teacup. Quietly, he walked across the room. He lifted his violin from the lid of his piano, drew his bow, and began to play the most spontaneous notes that had ever been played. The character closed his eyes; if it wasn't music as he knew it, it was something richer, stranger. Song sparrows? Marsh wrens?

Friend, said the man from the novel.

Friend, said the hermit, swallowing back tears.

Wait. I'm mixing up two stories here, *The Bride of Frankenstein* and who knows what else. And the woods are black, my flashlight's dead, and why is that deer chirruping up ahead?

Wait, says the hermit, playing up an octave.

Listen, says the man from the novel, reaching for a plate.

Yes? say I.

And for some years, the two live happily together in the woods.

ROPE BRIDGE

Bob got the urge to jump up and down on the rope bridge. Halfway out over the gushing creek—was that so strange? "Don't even think about it," said Pete, who opened his eyes long enough to see the pressure of holding it back trembling the corners of Bob's mouth.

But the shock of great height: could Pete pass some of that into Bob? And play: could Bob pass some of that into Pete? Maybe then they'd smell the water on the plants, taste the mist in their mouths. And Bob wouldn't have to shimmy ahead, swinging the bridge from side to side.

LIGHTEN UP, IT'S SUMMER!

The renters recline in their lounge chairs around the pool.
The heat's a little much. No wind shifts the leaves on the trees,
and who could blame anyone for staying in one place all day?
Hours must be filled, magazines flipped through and dropped.
Someone says *ass*, which brings on some laughs. Someone
says *Britney*, which brings on some more. Though none of the
laughter suggests the jokes are very funny, not that they're
supposed to be. The vodka gets stronger in the glasses. The
blue of the pool should shut up. The silence in the woods asks
something of them. That something might hurt, which is why
the pool speakers kick on, not just a little loud, but loud enough
to shake the minds of the people in the house next door, to let
everyone know they're here and have each other. It's not music
that anyone likes—that would be missing the point. Songs aren't
meant to be remembered late at night when you're trying to fall
asleep because, let's face it, time's an illusion that's meant to be
conquered. Someone says, *Lindsay Lohan.* Laughter vibrates in
six sets of vocal chords, in unison. *If it were up to me, I'd kill every
animal on this island!* And they go on like this and on like this.

All in a day's work, really, for it takes great energy and patience to drain yourself of feeling, to nod and blink exactly to your neighbor's rhythm.

A little past noon, a rustling inside the woods. A creature stands inside the clearing, hoof tapping the ground like some polished black boot. Phantom? Beast? No, deer—but not like the deer grazing the sides of the road. Hairy, thick through the ribs, he leaps over the bubbling hot tub, legs practically flying over their faces until he lands on the deck with a crack. Someone shrieks. They laugh, because they're afraid not to laugh. All that motion! That tail! Why them? Then he looks at their bare feet with a snort, turning his neck to the left before he's off again, out and away, nothing left of his presence but the faintest scent of barnyard and leaves.

The Now is what they're after. The Now tries very hard to hold on to what it has without breaking. The Now concentrates like a bead of rainwater, poised on the edge of a fig leaf, focusing itself so it won't fall into the pool.

Number 1 turns to Number 2: "Doesn't Kant say the mind

requires space and time in order to perceive?"

"Huh?" they all say at once.

"Listen," he says. "'What may be the nature of objects considered as things in themselves and without reference to the receptivity of our sensibility is quite unknown to us.'"

All five stare at Number 1 as if he's wearing last year's swimsuit. Inside out, no less.

"Lighten up," says Number 2.

"Yeah, right," says Number 3, turning over on his side. "It's summer."

The sun refuses movement. The heat's a little much. They go on like this and on like this.

Boys of shadow, boys of noon: who's the one who told you the self's just one more thing to lose?

BAMBOO

Across the way, the old man is at it again, cutting off stalks

with his shears. He pants and he sweats. His shoes are soaked

through. He smells like a goat when the wind hits him right.

That's right, like a petting zoo, all the way to here.

So what if they're sprouting in your yard and our yard?

Asparagus spears. Or weapons from some martial arts

extravaganza.

I wonder if the old men of China hate bamboo like that, Mark

says.

Or it's a body thing, I say. If you can't control the flow of your

bladder, or the hairs growing on your shoulders and your back...

And it's true. Every man I knew who hated bamboo had

had enough of all that. See them racing around town on their

motorcarts. Or pumping out crawlspaces, nailing on roofs.

This is not a story about dicks, if that's what you're thinking.

But the species is invasive, trills the naturalist from her bicycle.

And I'm much wilder than you think, I say.

All the while the old man's clippers go chop, chop, chop.

BAMBOO SPEAKS

Mind moving beneath the soil. Not a kind mind, but lovelier, and tricky, thinking in every direction. And more of life and more of life and more.

THE LITTLE SONGS

Three notes into the song, and I'm cooked. And I know myself
as well as I know the inner life of a sunflower stalk. You did
that, you know. Yesterday, in the woods, when you pointed out
the little songs I sing to myself when someone gets close to me.
I never knew that's what brought it on, just like I never knew
till now that you sing to keep yourself lifted when the light in
you wants to go down, down. Should I tell you that? Oops. But I
completely get it why any of us might need to say those are your
fingers, your shins, and your habits given the mighty temptation
to merge. Aren't those ducks on the waves a single circling braid,
and the gulls in the air another, clockwise against counter-
clockwise, as if every brain cell must be summoned to resist the
one great mass? And how many times a month do we hear, are
you guys related? No, we're from Fire Island, though I never find
the sass in me to say so. Damned if you do and damned if you
don't. So no wonder we make our self-blessings, these little fences
in notes, even as I catch our legs, in shadows, moving in single
step.

IN THE UNLIKELY EVENT

When I watched her teaching us the fundamentals of emergency crash position, I thought, this woman likes her movies too much. How else to account for the way she smiled through her tears? Why turn her back on us and sob into her fist? (I looked over my shoulder. Were we sure this wasn't being filmed? Allen Funt? Where on the plane was Allen Funt?) Nevertheless, I behaved as I was supposed to behave. I tried not to fuss; I tried not to make too much of the coiffed businesswoman to our left, who reached into the seat pocket in front of her, and with refinement and discretion, put her airsickness bag to good use. Surely, we'd land and clap and laugh at the whole damn thing. And it was only when Mark took my hand, the way others around us took their neighbors' hands, that I felt the surge of heartbreak, adrenaline, and embarrassment that lets us know we're not asleep.

How, then, in the time that followed, did I become someone I didn't know?

It wasn't wisdom. I had as much wisdom in my head as there were pain pills in my back pocket—which meant none. And it certainly wasn't cool. Even strapped in my seat and chastened,

I felt my left heel tapping out a warning code. Maybe some of
it had to do with the years I wouldn't get to live out with Mark.
The fun we'd miss. Our house. Our dogs. Who would watch over
our dogs? At least the two of us would go down at once, if that
was any kind of comfort. But what did comfort mean when Mark
looked so unguarded and hurt, as if he were determined to take
it personally, and couldn't foresee that he'd one day get a poem
out of the experience?

And here's where another stepped in. I wouldn't have believed
it either if you'd told me that my mother leapt up from her house
in Florida like some superhero ready to save the day. But there
she was, standing at the sink, running hot water over a jar she
couldn't open. And when I thought of her getting that phone call
the next morning, just as she wrenched off the lid, I numbed. Not
because she loved me better than anyone, or because I remotely
approximated the son she'd wanted me to be, but because she'd
had enough for one life. And the thought of making her suffer
(guilt! even in my last minutes above earth) was not something
I could take on right then. So my two legs pushed into the floor

as if it were possible to pilot the plane myself, even as the damn thing wobbled and swung, and the silos of the midwest looked nearer and nearer.

That's when I went through the window, the tiny square window to my right. Pinned to my seat, squeezing Mark's hand, I thought myself into that sky, taking myself out of the body that was sure to be pummeled and burnt. I was aware of my ability to influence, and not, and there was a calm to the procedure, like what it must feel to be an addict, on a good day, when you push your blood back and forth through the works. Was that why the treetops beneath us were greener than mangrove? Or why I could so readily think of each person who mattered, and put a hand on each forehead, and each face, as if I'd always been faithful to the God I'd prayed to as a child, but hadn't known that till now?

I thought some of that light into the head of each person on the plane—to Mark, to the flight attendant, even to the pilot, who must have been doing the best he could with the creature that was trying and failing to hold us aloft.

Not to mention my mother.

Maybe that's why we landed as smoothly as we did. Or I'm kidding myself, because just when it was clear that we were out of harm's way—though I'm not telling you the whole story; I'm leaving out firemen and ambulances and a line of tornadoes, too obscene to talk about—I felt something like rage as we waited to be transported by bus by members of the National Guard. Rage to be back in a body after the high of being out of it. Rage to realize I'd never outsmart death, though a part of me had tricked myself into thinking I'd passed some test.

MODERNISM

1. SPEEDBOAT

After Morris Lapidus' rendering of the International Trade Center

The speedboat I'm in barely makes a wake. The captain keeps his
clothes on. I don't mind standing beside him in this swimsuit,
because your eye goes only to the finger that's pointing ahead.
It was never about the buildings, though they're as shapely as
dresses. It was never about the plants and flags: they're only in
the way. It's what you can't see that makes you want it, which is
why you're relieved the dream stays just a dream. Isn't it better
that the bay we're passing through never burns our nostrils with
oil, never uglies our drinking supply, never rises higher than
the seawall, slopping the parks and lights and trees? Just a blue,
tranquil mirror intended to lengthen and stretch. Everything
poised on *becoming,* which is where we always wanted to be. And
though the palm beside us looks like it might murder us—Look!
Three times taller than the towers in the distance!—what it
wants of us is wonder: to empty us out that we might start all
over again.

2. TEARDOWN

When the woman at the fancy dinner dismissed the populist modernist houses that he so loved, she probably didn't know that she was committing murder. But if she did know, she did it with maximum efficiency, as if by taking down the glass walls, the posts and beams, the leafy atriums, she was dismantling everything they stood up against: darkness, meanness, the small constricted ways of the past. And just when he thought he couldn't stand it anymore, she let him know with a subtle smile that her sister had demolished one of those same houses to build a monster house—not that she called it that—to the consternation of her neighbors on the street.

3. A LITTLE MURDER

Years before my teenage brother had collected enough mid-century modern furniture to fill up a three-bedroom summerhouse and then some, he bought a small teak figure resembling a Nordic explorer. He was twelve then. It wasn't long before he'd outgrown such simple taste and advanced to the next level, sophistication the order of the day: McCobb, Bertoia, Eames, Finn Juhl. As if to prove this to my mother and me, he held the little man in the air, daring us to stop him. His smile pulled in four directions at once: part triumph, part despair, part relief, part hatred. But in spite of our cries, he slammed the man against the wall. And when that didn't do it, he slammed it once again. We watched in awe as the man broke apart, the shiny wooden head rolling to the corner of the room. The house went quiet. Outside, beside the dock, an egret gave a little laugh. How could we be connected to something so spoiled and sick? What was ahead for us? We couldn't yet see that he needed to get it first before it got him, which is the way we are with perfection.

THE POODLES OF MY CHILDHOOD

The poodles of my childhood were nothing like the poodles of
today. Wooly and dry, they looked unkempt, unclean. And when
you tried to pet them, as you were told children were supposed
to do, they reared, whimpered, and turned their pretty heads.
When it was time to do their business, they didn't walk off to a
corner, or cower behind a bush, but did it right on your father's
grass, no thought as to whether it should be beside the lamppost
or the fencepost, and they faced you as they squatted, daring
you to react. In days you'd go out back, looking for what they'd
left behind, but it was never what you'd imagined. Stones, a
paste of chewed leaves, used charcoal. When you thought about
what came out of you, it was nothing like that. You would have
stopped it if it had even been an option, just like you stopped
up your ears when the street cleaner roared, or pulled down the
shade to block out the face of the moon. Terrible moon, until you
renamed her Melissa, so she'd appear friendly and kind, and you
could finally sleep in your bed without trembling or pressing
your fists to your eyes.

Which might have had something to do with the lemonade

stand you'd set up by the street. Something to give you courage, though you never cared very much about courage. No one had stopped for lemonade all day, not that you didn't want it that way. Then who could that be but the Hussman girl coming toward you with one of those poodles? You reached for the sign: *No Sale!* And you couldn't even look at her soft freckled arms, without thinking of the Hussman girl's older sister, who fell back, threw up, and died, in kindergarten, as she cut out a drawing of the human heart. That was how they always said it, the same sequence: she fell back, threw up, and died, pulling the piece of construction paper with her. There you stood with no place to go, and there the Hussman girl came toward you with hunger and interest on her face, and you felt the back of her sister's head slam the tile, heard the children leap up and laugh, thinking it was a joke, and what could you do but fall to the grass yourself? Not that you really fell down, not exactly, but you knelt behind your stand and covered your head with the sign. And what did she do, but let her dog squat not ten feet from you. She smiled, nodding at the poodle's trembling hind legs as if all were right and good, and turned, without as much as a wave, and walked back down the sidewalk toward her house, humming faintly.

You walked toward what came out of the dog. It was last you'd see of it like this. Fresh and glistening, nestled in its bed of grass.

"She let her dog poop on our yard!"

Dinnertime. You tried as hard as you could to keep it inside but the more you tried, the more your news wanted to be said.

"Who, dear," your mother said.

It was the night of white food: creamed cauliflower, mashed potatoes, cod. She sat perfectly straight as she lifted a slab of fish to your plate.

"The Hussman girl."

"Where?" your father said.

You told him exactly where he could find it: by the lamppost, but not by one of the fenceposts.

"And you told her to pick it up?" he said.

But he wouldn't look at you. His knife sawed through the fish, and just by the way he worked it back and forth, with such fantastic love and care, you knew he knew you'd never surprise him.

"Her sister died," you mumbled into your hands.

"And I work hard on my lawn." He eased back from the table and carried his plate to the sink, where he dumped it over the drain cover. He turned. But the look on his face was not a look familiar to you. It looked reddish and scared, eyes off to one side.

Of course there was another day. You'd already given up your lemonade stand, handed the pitcher back to your mother. Maybe if you stayed inside the Hussman girl would never find you again, and there'd be good enough reason to take the dog down a different street. You built a fort of towels and sheets inside your bedroom, cooked paper burgers atop a shoebox, seasoning them with glitter. Still, you couldn't stop from sneaking looks out your window, and every time you did so, you wondered whether you were making an ending come closer, and the next time you went into your backyard you saw how many times the dog had come to see you. Not once, twice, but three times, until you nearly fell down from the counting.

Your father stood with you on the yard. What had come out of the dog had washed away in the rain, but there were rings now, the color of coffee grounds, staining his good grass.

"Didn't you tell her to pick it up?"

His eyes focused in the distance like they were seeing something. He handed you the shovel without looking in your direction.

"No," you mumbled.

"What's the matter?" your father said. "Are you a fraidy-boy?"

Annnnnh, you shrieked, with a sound like a crow.

And what of the *you* here? Did you actually believe the second-person would make you stronger, would help you save them?

Think again.

MR. CAT

Would it ever occur to you to drive the wrong way into a traffic circle?

Fifteen cents for the winning answer.

Honestly, I *believed* my father when he said he'd been lost in thought, and had forgotten too late that one went right instead of left. Never mind that he'd been driving this circle for 19 of his 36 years. Never mind the oncoming streams of jeeps, boat trailers, and beach buggies. Am I asking for too much when I propose he was giving us the bones of something we could give flesh to in another life? Life after life—and, oh, the grand dinners beside the littered shore! And oh, the trips given up on two miles before the tip of the continent! Who could ever say what childhood was from here, what it felt like to be caught up inside the mouth of it?

Outside on the woodpile, a cat looks satisfied and suspicious. From his mouth, the wiry tail switches left, right, left, right, and relaxes. The cat blinks, but I know what that mouse is thinking: it isn't so bad in here. Maybe I could put up drapes, hang up calendars, find me a pole lamp. And *hobbies!*

And he's too caught up in his glee to see the muscles already working in that extraordinary throat.

LOVE STORY

The lights went down. The heating system hushed. The man
behind us pushed his hand inside his popcorn barrel, but did
I take in the sound? I didn't take in the sound. I was too busy
concentrating on the figures up there, a man and a woman
whose shouting matches made as much sense to me as the boys
and the girls who had sex in the woods.

My mother's arm leaned into my arm, her bare skin thinking,
shifting, as if there were a mind in it. Was I seeing what she'd
wanted me to see? "I have to take him to the movie," she'd said
yesterday, a little shy, defeated, to her friend. "Maybe then he'd
put some feeling into it." She was talking about my school solo
of course, which was coming up in a week. I went on practicing
as if I hadn't heard her through the wall. The metronome
clicked; the songbook slid off the rack onto my hands, the floor.
I couldn't figure out why it wasn't enough to play the notes
right. Not enough to keep the tempo steady, not enough to
press and release the pedal at the end of each measure. I was
holding the song like a house in my hands, but feeling? What
was feeling? When I thought of feeling I thought of all the things

I wasn't supposed to think. I thought of my grandmother, and her mother: hard dry loaves turning to stone in the ground. Or worse, what I did late at night. Headlight patterns fell like screens down the wall. The man from the movie leaned down, warmed my face with his mouth, just as he'd warmed the face of the dying girl to send her off for the night. And in that moment when I'd expected to find tears on my pajamas—yes, tears, would this be the night?—all I felt was dry.

At the concert I played as I'd always played. All the sharps were sharp, all the flats flat, and the pacing? As steady as the metronome on the piano back at home. The audience went away. Even I went away. All that was left of us was sound, one note leading into the next, as if music built a pathway into the thicket. We saw it ahead of us: a cold dank woods with Kleenexes on the ground. The concert hall went dark. The exit sign switched off. We grew taller, each of us swelling to the size of actors on a screen. We imagined ourselves touched, not by our own hands, but by those who wanted to know us, remember us. We didn't cover our faces. And when I stood up to take in their applause—

Were those tears in my pants? Of course not, but something had changed, even if I was only dreaming the wet down there.

"That was beautiful," my mother's friend said afterward. "Look at me," she said, "I still have tears in my eyes."

"Did you hear that?" my mother said. "Did you say thank you?"

But her face told me that feeling was on the other side of those woods.

THE PILLORY

A replica of a pillory in a replica of a Colonial town. My right arm into the right hole, my left arm into the left. My neck went right through the center. I laughed, not because there was anything funny about being hung up on a cross, but just because it felt good to be away from home, school. The marketplace steamed with activity. The worn patch of grass beside the horseblock, the boxwoods by the cobbler's shop, the flies buzzing above the tidy piles of dung. And it wasn't any wonder that the faces before me receded in the glare. It wasn't any wonder that I stopped thinking of my mother and her neck aches, or my father and his call for constant motion whenever he was home from work, even though we never got anything done.

I didn't think of the other boys once punished like that. I didn't give a thought to the eggs, fruit, mice, and shit thrown at their faces. *There can be no outrage more flagrant,* Hawthorne said, *than to forbid the culprit to hide his face for shame.* But was it shame I felt? I only knew that I was tired of holding myself up. I wanted to cave in and so I caved in. Which was why, after I'd grown used to my new position, I pulled myself out and forgot I had a body.

Or took three steps backward and fell a hard five feet to the ground.

It wasn't me, then, that dropped like a bale of hay from a burning barn. It wasn't me lying on my back as the crowd looked on. Or me, for that matter, covering my crotch with my hand, as if I'd already known that they were hungry for murder.

A little girl screamed, and I was relieved to hear that scream tear through the heat.

Relieved, too, to hear my father walking out of the crowd. Relieved to see the arm he raised, for wasn't that him reaching out to help me up? No, that was the crowd in that arm—I can only see it from here—and he was setting his face for what he didn't want to do, which was to spank me as one spanks an errant child, not a 12-year old boy whose voice was on the verge of changing.

Once, twice: who can remember such things? Did I feel it? Did I send myself away? He hit me as the crowd looked on, even as his eyes said, who am I doing this for? Aren't you my son? He stopped and he blinked, as if he hadn't known where he'd gone.

Then led me to a tool shed on the periphery, where he cleaned off my knee with a handkerchief he'd pulled from his pocket.

I don't have to say that I spent the rest of the day swimming back and forth across the motel pool until the chlorine stung. I got up. I got up in the way we all get up against the arm that wants to keep us down.

Maybe that's what my father already knew back then. And maybe that's why he brought it up at the dinner table thirty years later, though I'd forgotten it, as I'd forgotten many things by then. His eyes looked through me, past me. He spoke as if that memory were just one more thing he'd been wearing around his neck, and the straight-ahead gaze it required of him was no longer serving him at this late hour, what with the bills stacking up on his desk, my mother in Ranmar Gardens, and the empty rooms of the apartment that needed cleaning.

Which was why I didn't throw the balled-up napkin in my hand, though I'd be lying if I didn't admit to that temptation. I put my hand over my father's. And looked away from the face that didn't need my forgiveness.

THE LINE IT DREW

"We won't notice a thing," said my father to the woman next door.

The tops of the pitch pines stilled. I waited for those words to shudder through him, through my neighbor. Around the eyes, the lips, a little twitch, whatever. Instead, they shuddered through me. My face grew hot, hotter. I closed my mouth so nothing would come out like that. I kept it closed for years.

Late that night, beneath the screen window, I concentrated on the part that would soon be cut from her, shivering on aluminum in the operating room. Gleaming and real: too much life for the body it had wanted to escape. I put my hand on my chest, thought of the scalpel, the line it drew. Fever and its aromas. Then the darkness that could come out if I had that hole in me.

Did my father know he should have kept those words inside?

Did my neighbor?

And from then on, I couldn't keep my eyes from drifting to where they weren't supposed to be.

nose, maybe because she couldn't stop looking at us. She didn't seem to worry that her mother was probably taking the long, pretty way to school, beneath the elms, past the creek where the water smelled rotten, like food. She didn't seem to worry about what we'd say outside. Lily had her sandwich, after all, which lasted all day in her hand. And the children, of course, who were nothing more than the moving figures of her attention.

She knew she'd changed everything in that room. It was hers now. She was the queen of it, and more.

My brother? He disappeared, a little at a time, until all that was left was a sweater, a nest of fuzz and hair and threads. We gave them everything they asked for. We were good that way.

THE PISS OF NEW YORK

July 2007

We always thought it was permanent. The smell of sidewalk, ripe
and true the second summer rolled around. And whether it got
there through dog, person, or alien from outer space was beside
the point. You either had to say, ah, New York, or take your
opinions elsewhere. Besides, wasn't it a freakish night, and who
knew what wonder we'd careen into up ahead?

And now? I don't need to belabor the point. It's stupid to
bemoan something just because it isn't there. And even if it
was, I'm sure those with the guidebooks wouldn't even be able
to smell it if it wasn't approved of first. Oh, there I go again.
Let them have their joy. Let them marvel that they're not being
mugged, that we have the same stores they have, that they can
walk down the street, behave exactly as they want to, and feel
they're in a movie. Anyway, let's be clear: who among us isn't up
there, on the upper deck of those tour buses, looking down, or
maybe not, to see what we can see?

And up from the subway deep comes the creature of the
night: half woman, half man, dressed head to toe in pink. Pink

tracksuit, pink lips, pink brows arched high above the ravenous

eyes. Seventy-five feet tall, though no one can yet discern the

tugboat features. And from its moving mouth comes the gruff,

correcting message: *I am always greater than you. Watch me eat.*

And throws an armload of us down on the sidewalks we thought

clean.

VERY GOOD

Very Good will not do for her. A plate of pudding; pajamas
slipped into on a winter night: those are Very Good, but not
writing. Very Good is never writing, not if she has a hand in
it. But Very Good was how the reader responded to her stories,
and though she knows too well the costs of wanting, she goes
through the next hour with her shoulders slumped and her arms
folded down at her waist. The very notion of Very Good: Very
Good doesn't get its pants dirty. Very Good doesn't take its pants
down, or even off. It's always hiking them up too high, and when
she wants it to roll around in bed with her, it sits on the other
side of the room, with pleasant smile and peppermint breath,
and keeps her up all night with the books it had been meaning
to write if only it had had the time. As if all she had were time
and a life in which the sentences came at her like kisses, or hard
little fucks. She should put it out of its misery, that Very Good.
She should shoot Very Good in the foot, or yank that foot out of
its mouth. But Very Good does not feel enough to feel misery.
Very Good is too concerned for its own safety to take note of the
sweat, the shit, and the tears.

And on the other side of the city, her reader sits with the writer's pages opened upon his lap. Now he thinks he should have told her the truth: that her stories held him down when he thought he'd rise up off the earth. And when we went back to the book and reread a passage about snow, he felt it as if it were his snow, but better, burning the sleeping parts of him awake. But did he tell her that? No. He knows down deep the costs of wanting, the hothouse word that chills the plant at the root. Very Good is plenty and exact and oh so still in the face of what he loves.

Meanwhile, across the city, the writer throws forks at the two sheets of paper she's taped to the kitchen wall.

And a Very Good wind is lost inside the spaces between words.

THE MOTHER TONGUE

On a morning like this morning, who could blame you for
twisting inside your sweater, pushing your husband aside, and
walking the six flights down to the lobby to wait for the bus to
take you to Mother's. There is no bus, Mom. And Mother? Well,
you yourself called three years ago, at ten o'clock on a Tuesday
night, crying, to let me know she'd died, even though history
tells us it was 1960, when she gave up after you'd gotten married
and had a son. I'm sorry for my lack of reaction. I think you
know a whole lot more than you let on, but the Mother Tongue
is more than we can take today. Mother has a smile as wide as
Seattle. Mother can speak and write 127 languages, including
Danish and Japanese. Mother once carried a grand piano on her
shoulders all the way to Africa and back in addition to bringing
peace to all peoples, curing impetigo, and helping the children.
Mother, Mother, and more Mother. We get it, all right? And if you
need to go back? No one's stopping you here. Back to the little
farm off the White Horse Pike, back to the cats and grammar
school, back to the chocolate eggs you stole one Easter, and all
you could have been before chance and will took us forth from

you and into the world. Go, I'm not afraid. But if Mother should be hard to find, or if you don't think she knows the girl you are in the car coat and beanie, keep this in mind: There might just be a future you didn't want to walk away from.

THE SUPERMARKET OF OUR CHILDHOOD

When you lost what you remembered, we lost each other

too. By which I mean the brothers who depended upon each

another for laughs went their different ways, as if we couldn't

bear to be reminded of the hole of where you were. Who knew

you were the ground we walked on, dreamed on? And all the

arcane references somehow led back to you, where you once sat

on the lawn chair, beaming, like the great Mama bird outside

Wanamakers. Now the backyard where you watched us is

choked with bamboo, and the jokes we told at your expense?

At least they brought a smile to your face, which was why we

made them up in the first place. Name one cashier from the

supermarket of our childhood, says my brother today. And

though I know he's obsessed with memory tests, I deliberately

give him the name of the late family dog. Well, let me reserve a

deluxe private suite at the nursing home, he says. Pack your hat.

And forgetfulness, for just a second, doesn't look like the worst

place to be.

IRREVERENCE

Three brothers huddled near the aunt's furnace, making fun
of their grandmother. They pulled out a piece of chalk and
scratched their names into the floor. Above, the father walked
from breadbox to refrigerator, with no clue as to the wretched
things spoken in the basement.

It wasn't that they disliked their grandmother. In their brighter
moments they thought of her as a gentle, befuddled moose, far
from her natural habitat, her mouth full of leaves. At other times?
We won't speak of them here. She simply made no sense to them,
especially as the receptacle of so much affection. Had she ever
forgotten to put vinegar on the father's fish? Was there ever a
day when she looked more favorably on his left ear than his
right? The father's love left no room for answers, as if any sign
of trouble got in the way of devotion. And what of the way he
looked at her? Well, let's just say they ran out of the house each
time they saw it, especially because he'd never smiled at their
own mother like that.

Over time, the grandmother grew larger with love. Love
pinned her to the sofa. Love made sure she didn't have to speak,

or lift her knife and fork, or cut her meat. Love swelled her the way a tree given too much light, water, and fertilizer grows to improbable proportions, which in turn makes its leaves spot and fall as the flies hover about its trunk.

"A solar eclipse will blot out the sun," said Brother #1.

"The velvet curtain will rip in half in the sanctuary," said Brother #2.

"What about this," said Brother #3. "The moon will rise in blood?"

The brothers didn't shudder, nor did they throw themselves face down on the floor, banging with their fists. It had seemed like a good idea to strike out at the most hallowed thing they could think of: God's reaction to the moment of their grandmother's death. But it didn't give them the satisfaction they'd been dreaming of. They sat there, heads down, chastened by the footsteps above, and holding back the thing they feared most: that once she died—and she was certain to, any day now, though the dying had been taking years—they'd lose their father to grief.

When they looked down, a cold clear drop of water rolled across the basement floor.

No curtain tore the night the grandmother died. No ash fell on the porch. The moon, when the brothers looked out the window, barely made it higher than the snowy rooftops before it set. But when the father came down to the kitchen the next morning to pour his cereal into a bowl, they were relieved to hear him talking about putting on an extra story to the house. Maybe even building a maze in the backyard. Their lives would go on as usual, just as their mother had said they would. Still, they couldn't help but feel cheated out of something large, though they didn't quite know what it was.

During the funeral the choir sang badly as if they'd sung what they sang a thousand times. The father was fine and then he wasn't. When the brothers could no longer bear the sounds and sights around them, they lifted themselves out of their seats and swooped aloft, high above the mourners in the pews. They flew about the rafters, safe there, like mice with wings on their backs.

If they'd been paying attention to what they could see from

those heights, they'd have seen that mothers deserved the chance to move, that if we loved them properly, with just the right degree of distance, we'd give them our blessing to go on to the next thing and forget us. Instead, they chose to refuse that little bit of knowledge. They landed back down in their seats, where they listened to the hymn the choir ruined, which they made fun of sometime later before they stopped that kind of thing.

THE DIDACHE

What were you like the last time I saw you whole? I know
nothing is as simple as whole versus broken, such as what we
were once told about the bread of God, but what did you have
on? The blouse with the anchor on the front? Which watch? And
had you colored your hair with the summer ash you'd sworn
by for so long? Maybe it was the day you stood at the kitchen
counter, and you made me a sandwich and I let you do it, even
though I was a guest in your house, and I was perfectly capable
of making my own. I think now about how proud you were to
put it together, as if it took an effort you used to take for granted:
the sliced ham atop the slice of white bread, the Miracle Whip,
the torn wet lettuce leaf, the kind of sandwich we don't even
eat anymore, though you put it in my lunch bag for years. It's
funny how we end up where we do. There you are in the state
whose name you wouldn't even consider without saying *too hot*
or *hurricanes*. And I was practically—a business major? Good
God, leave it to you to figure out at the last minute that I was
only trying to win you, though I couldn't yet see it for myself.
And you said *writing*—and thereby saved me. I've never told

you that. It's fashionable to say that words, among other things, fail us, and mostly I think that's true, but what would I be if I couldn't set this down? As the broken bread was scattered on the hillsides, and so was gathered and made one, so may the many of you be gathered and find favor with one another. And even if wholeness is ridiculous to expect at this late stage of the story, well? *At least you're still around,* says the business major who never got to be. *Take. Eat,* says the mother, given up and broken, and pushes the sandwich into the lunch bag, and sends me on my way.

BRACELET

"Here is your bracelet," says the nurse, snapping the plastic shut around what's left of my mother's wrist. "This is your identity. You're not allowed to take this off."

"Even into death?" my mother says, bemused. And not.

The nurse, whom I haven't made eye contact with, because I've been trying not to hate that another-old-white-woman-to-put-up-with tone of hers, stops. Literally. As if she can actually hear the footsteps down to surgery. And lifts her face. As the two of us laugh away our shock, which is to say the truth the living can never get behind.

"You're not dying," the nurse and I say now, almost at the same time. "No, no, no, no, no, no, no. Not today."

We're grinning now, in the manner of old friends, our relationship stronger for having passed a trinket back and forth, and seen it shine, and known, between us, how much it needed to be put away.

"What's your relationship to the patient?" she says softly, wiping my mother's lip with the sponge.

"I'm her son," I say. "Her oldest."

And the surprise on my mother's face! Into a new room, into an old sentence whose structure you could never complete.

"Yay!" we all say.

And the stain of light on our tongues.

TOO LATE FOR A GOOD WINK

The sky shat snow some more, and the coffee shop's a colloquy
of the damaged, and in comes Choo Choo, the wide-assed
wonder, to wipe off his tiny spectacular feet. Oral B.'s tugging
at the waistband of the loveliest sweatpants this side of the
Great Lakes, and what? I'm sounding more like Denis Johnson
than I've ever sounded like myself. Just another butt day at the
margins of the world. Is it any wonder that we feel like we feel
when they put the Adult Book Gallery dead smack in the center
of things, high inside the choir loft of the First Church of Christ,
and even the fratboys drop their irony in the mud at the bottom
of the lake. The trick is to keep on laughing. You said it yourself
when you said it was too late for a good wink, then proceeded to
go ahead and do so. Expertly, I might add. Mother, my name is
Paul, and though we once had more than a passing acquaintance,
we lost ourselves along the way, far from our vivid ocean, on the
bus route northeast of Owego. The right hand doesn't talk to the
left. Nothing we do appears to matter, and when we try to make
it to the end of the sentence and can't, we get indulged for it.
Of course you're a little frozen, their faces try to tell us, because

we brought you here. Frankly, I'd prefer some censure, a kick in the pants, an old fashioned slap upside the head, but good luck getting anyone to see us. In the meantime we have these balls of solder rolling around inside our brains. Are you with me? The lights turn off in the valley, one by one by one. Heat's something we could use a little more of, what with words that far away.

ON THE TABLE

Well into the second half-hour of the massage, just as Lou pushes my bent left leg into my chest, I think with interest, and maybe a little sadness, that I don't lose it as much as I used to. It's not that Lou isn't the best at what he does—my hand flops off the table like a puppet's—but where's the kind of swimming through space that I once described with such faith? I'm talking about that scene when the character gives in to those hands on him, just after he's decided to tell the guy who's rubbing his back he doesn't want to see him anymore. Today that moment strikes me as heightened, further evidence of the desire for transcendence I've always been more compelled by than I'd like to be. As Lou takes hold of my left foot and rotates it gently, in a half-circle, I give myself permission to say that I've failed, the kind of thing all artists try on from time to time, or maybe more, and you know what? It could be worse. I mean, there's time. And if not, someone else will do my work for me—and better. Then just when I've resigned myself to a life in which I'll never again lose my composure, even though I've written a few books that have more to do with early Laura Nyro and probably Courtney Love than the person I've become, I say to myself, *ah, what it means to grow older.* And that makes me remember you—*you!*—and how much you liked human hands rubbing your paws and muzzle and tail. Wasn't it just a few days back when was I telling myself I don't think about you so much anymore? It felt okay to admit to that, as if that's what you'd wanted for me, really, in spite of those tiresome pleas for attention: to go on to the next day, without being stopped by the sight of another who moved along with your sideways gimp. And that's you, isn't it, in the groan that comes from way down deep in my ribcage. You when I shift a little on the table and sigh through the nostrils, in relief. Lou's hands on your lower leg, Lou in your arthritic joints until there's no me left, only your old happiness, plain and grateful. I'm so glad he's here for you. A woman I know writes about her bird, who died at the vet's yesterday after going in to get her beak trimmed: "When it's that easy for a life to disappear, it's a little hard to believe that it's ever been there at all." And don't I know that from where I am? Well, I shouldn't presume. Though there's more to say about art and the desire for transcendence, and the virtues of *Suddenly Last Summer* and Maria Callas's self-punishing performance in *Norma*, I'll step out of the skin of the story and give you center stage, Arden, the place you'd always wanted, though you were content to stay on the sidelines. It's enough to know what you felt like, even if I won't a minute from now, when I put my clothes back on. Then Lou places a dry kiss on top of—whose head? And there's laughter in the room, your old smell of corn muffins and soot.

FACE

I'm running in the dunes around a big beach house, in a place
that looks like Cape May, though it isn't Cape May. I'm in with a
pack of my kind. Twelve retrievers, all of the same size. Our coats
are glossy and clean. Our lungs are large, as open as suitcases.
Just to think I'll never be a burden again! I'd love to pull you all
the way down to the bay till the leash blisters your hand.

Even I'd almost forgotten that I was ever young.

I speak from some distant future, yours and mine.

Still, it's not exactly heaven. I miss a piping cold morning: the
hard divide between day and night. (That's the payback for never
having to die again, this middling state where the light stays the
same). And the food's a little wholesome. I'd give anything to
come upon a dropped frankfurter (*not* hot dog), seasoned with
pencil shaving, cobweb, and rock salt. But nothing was ever
perfect. As always, we make the best of our lot.

A ball is flung in our direction. It happens again and again.
One of us gets it, brings it back, only for the whole thing to start
all over again. It's never me who brings it back. Better to cheer
on the others. Unlike the others, I'm not interested in the ball. I

93

look for the face of the one who's throwing the ball, but there's nothing to look for. I'm not talking about some sleek, headless phantom. Yes, there are lips and moles. Yes, there are eyes, but they all have the same earnest, benevolent cast. I'll say it right here: the human face is often lowly, marred by lines and sags. It doesn't age as well as ours. And it's nude, right out there, the worst examples as pink as the skin of our private parts. Still, there's nothing lovelier, more rapturous than gazing into an actual human face. The quirk of an eyebrow, the watery glaze around the pulsating iris. The upper lip raised in anger. The mouth pushed out in a sideways funnel. There's nothing more pleasing than determining your wishes before you're even aware of them yourself. There's an art to this, of course, a rigor. Let down our guard, and before we know it, we're lost. Too easy to get swallowed up inside the storms behind your face. Before long we're feeling your sorrow and agitation. We're crying for you, only to make matters worse, because you're thinking, *why are you weeping when it's your work to make me feel better?*

I never wanted to kiss it, though. Your face, I mean. Believe me, there were plenty who tried to get me to kiss the human face, but I politely declined. I loved it with all my heart. I loved it even more than my own handsome face, even when I was slapped on the muzzle, or ordered to bed before I was tired, when all I wanted was to stay with you, my head on my paws beside your shoes, while the laughter went on all around us, and the cigarette smoke stung the linings of my nose, making it run.

Smells. I miss them too, while we're on that. Since time isn't a problem here, nothing rots. It might as well be the salad compartment inside a refrigerator. Here's something I'd trade for my newfound motion any day: the smell of a dead flounder on the beach, just as it's been ripened by the sun, set on by flies.

MOTHERS IN THE TREES

Most often we rush beneath them, thinking only of the rabbits who bounce away when they see us coming. But raise your head sometime. Whole households live up there, old mothers, young mothers, in-between mothers, always watching, always making sure we wear our windbreakers, or rinse our cups, or dowse the fires we start in the marshes. Every once in a while one comes down in the form of a bear, and we hide inside our bathrooms, trembling as she looks for sweets in our trash.

TWO GUYS

When you lost what you remembered, New Jersey became as
tired as they said it was, and childhood sprang traps, ready to
bite into the skin of our ankles. Will we get it back? Maybe it's
a relief that we've left it behind, and we can both give thanks
for this bout of forgetfulness. I never really missed Two Guys as
much as I missed you. The automatic doors, the trading stamps,
the blinding interior, monstrous as a spaceship: you deserve
better than nostalgia. There's always more to give our lives to,
even if we thought we'd landed at the end of the world. May
the stores be better where you are. May you not waste a single
second thinking about what you should or shouldn't buy. And
if you should hear a boy calling for his mother by the record
department, walk on. He's doing much better than you think,
really. He owes you that. The songs are blue and glistening, even
if he has a hard time making sense of them from here.

FICTIONEER

In the Not-Writing, he had a notion: he needed to protect time in order to make life.

But the Life-Made always wanted to stop before he did. The knife lifting above the cutting board, and wouldn't it rather be suspended, mid-gesture, before the pepper beneath it was split? At least that's what the story thought. It never wanted to be taken through the expected turns, to face the logic it was supposed to face. Every reason, then, for him to listen and listen until it tired him. Somewhere, out there, there was music. And his ears filled up with weeds.

No surprise, then, that the Flirtatious Puppet shook this way and that, sang *Come buy my meat, taste this little bit of mine,* and *why not take a walk with the pirates?*

But I have to make life in the morning, said the Fictioneer.

If you don't live it, said the Puppet, it won't come out your horn.

Oh, you didn't make that up.

And the Fictioneer lay back on his raft, dreaming as if he'd found himself on a sea in which there was no one to miss, and no one to miss him back.

But who am I if I can't trap time? he said, springing up from sleep. What will I be after I'm gone? Give me my edges, my boundaries!

And here the Puppet kissed his brow for good luck and tossed itself to the sharks.

FIRST BIRTHDAY

War in the news. Hunger in the news.

What of the following could stand up to that?

The waitress sits down the plates. Car noise rolls in from the street. The rotisserie chicken so spicy and sweet, my eyes water. After I finish my own plate, I start eating off of Mark's. The waitress walks by, laughs as if startled to see what she never thought she'd see. I cringe, blush, though I go right on stabbing at his plate. Over and over, I lift the fork to my mouth, shameless.

Around the corner to the nursery. Aisle after pleasantly messy aisle of sedum, spiral rush, mugo pine, more sedum. High sun on my forehead, seabreeze on my arms, legs, chest . . . . The weather of my childhood, the weather of the shore house. *(She came back.)* Then it occurs to me: so this is what it's like to be alive again. It hadn't even occurred to me I hadn't been alive.

Yesterday just happened to be her birthday. My mother's first birthday since the morning of her death.

BUNNY

Yesterday I opened the door of the big blue cabinet. Varnishy, rich: the indescribable smell of our black and white cat, Portia, who'd hid in there in the last weeks of her life, on a shelf behind CDs. Could it still smell of her after all these years? Nine years. She'd died in there, at some point when we were out for an afternoon.

I went for a bike ride. To my right, a square of grass vibrated on someone's lawn: raw green, bleached out, almost too much to look at. A bunny froze on the edge of that square, waiting. I had a notion that my mother was relieved to get back the part of herself that could worry about me again. Then the bunny ran.

THE MOTHER SITS DOWN ON THE BED

The mother sits down on the bed. She has just come back from checking on the sons whose throats were stuck with thoughts of her. They seemed to her in constant motion, one laying down cork, another practicing an English horn, a third trying and failing to write of her, as if by capturing her walk, or the wobble of her hello, he'd be doing a little something to bring her back. But she should talk. It is hard work to be dead. She should have been in training for this, instead of putting her feet up in front of the TV, eating crackers.

The fields of the earth are full of nests, and when a tractor goes by the eggs in the nests crack open, as if the birds inside their shells cannot stand the rumble one more minute. They want to fly and they're tired of being warmed. But the mother is grateful to be away from all that. The earth buzzes with noise and shoots push up through the festive green. Do not pause, my lovelies. Still, her urge to cool down their faces does not match her urge to stay where she is.